For my father, Roger, who was born during a blizzard —K.S.

To Howie and his first snowsuit —S.J.

Text copyright © 2022 by Kristen Schroeder

Jacket art and interior illustrations copyright © 2022 by Sarah Jacoby

Visit us on the Web! rhcbooks.com

Educators and librarians, for a variety of teaching tools, visit us at RHTeachersLibrarians.com

Library of Congress Cataloging-in-Publication Data

Names: Schroeder, Kristen, author. | Jacoby, Sarah (Illustrator) illustrator. • Title: So much snow / Kristen Schroeder ; [illustrated by] Sarah Jacoby. • Description: First edition. | New York : Random House Studio, [2022] | Audience: Ages 3–7. | Audience: Grades K–1. | Summary: Seven forest creatures, from a tiny mouse to a giant moose, hunker down in a snowstorm as they wonder when the snow will stop. • Identifiers: LCCN 2021049157 (print) | LCCN 2021049158 (ebook) | ISBN 978-0-593-30820-2 (hardcover) | ISBN 978-0-593-30821-9 (lib. bdg.) | ISBN 978-0-593-30822-6 (ebook) • Subjects: CYAC: Snow—Fiction. | Forest animals—Fiction. • Classification: LCC PZ7.1.S336545 So 2022 (print) | LCC PZ7.1.S336545 (ebook) | DDC [E]—dc23

The text of this book is set in 22-point Adobe Caslon.

The artist used watercolor, chalky pastel, and Photoshop magic to create the illustrations for this book.

Interior design by Rachael Cole

MANUFACTURED IN CHINA

10 9 8 7 6 5 4 3 2 1

First Edition

SO MUCH SNOW

written by

KRISTEN SCHROEDER

illustrated by

SARAH JACOBY

RANDOM HOUSE STUDIO · NEW YORK

On Monday, it starts to snow.

Silent swirling.

How high will it go?

On Tuesday, we get more snow.

Flakes floating.

How high will it go?

On Wednesday, *still* more snow.

Peaceful piling.

How high will it go?

On Thursday, the snow doesn't slow.
Fields filling.

How high will it go?

On Friday,

snow,

snow,

SNOW!

Hilltops hiding.

How high will it go?

On Saturday, cold winds blow.

Drifts dancing.

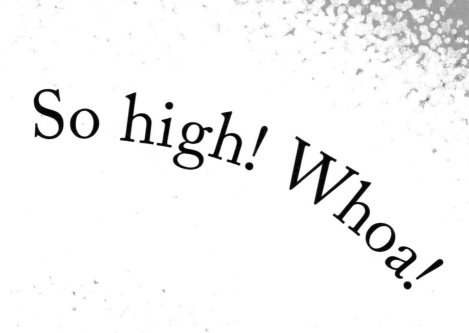

So high! Whoa!

On Sunday, the end of the snow.
Brilliant blanketing.

SO MUCH SNOW!

When will it go?

On Monday, the sun starts to show.

Mountains melting.

Look, it's Moose.

Hello!

Tuesday: two sunny days in a row.

Shapes shrinking.

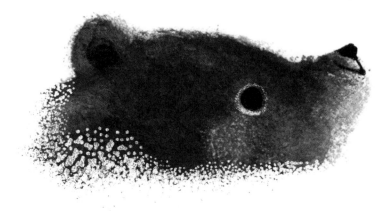

Oh, it's Bear. Hello!

On Wednesday, temperatures grow.

Things thawing.

I spy Deer. Hello!

On Thursday, rain melts snow.

Slush sliding.

Why, it's Wolf. Hello!

By Friday, streams begin to flow.

Prairies puddling.

I see Fox. Hello!

On Saturday, snow's new low.

White waning.

And there's Rabbit.

Hello!

It's Sunday. Where did it go?

Grass greening.

Hello, Mouse.

Hello!

NO MORE SNOW!

Trees budding,
birds singing,
everyone's springing.

But wait!

Is that . . . SNOW?!